Style trix

for COOL CHIX

your one-stop guide to finding the perfect look

Leanne Warrick

Watson-Guptill Publications/New York

First published in the United States in 2005 by
Watson-Guptill Publications,
a division of VNU Business Media, Inc.
770 Broadway, New York, NY 10003
www.wgpub.com

Produced by Breslich & Foss Ltd, London
Designed by Roger Daniels

Copyright © 2005 Breslich & Foss Ltd
Illustrations by Debbie Boon
Text by Leanne Warrick
Photos by Shona Wood

Special thanks to the cool chix in Watson-Guptill's teen focus group for their ideas, feedback,
and enthusiasm.

Library of Congress Control Number: 2004117688
Printed and bound in China

ISBN 0-8230-4940-X

2 3 4 5 6 7 8 / 12 11 10 09 08 07 06

Every effort has been made to ensure that the information presented is accurate. Readers
are strongly advised to read product labels, follow manufacturers' instructions, and heed
warnings. The publisher disclaims any liability for injuries, losses, untoward results, or any
other damages that may result from the use of the information in this book.

Contents

Ready

It's no secret that lots of girls love clothes, and why not? Who doesn't want to look her best? We all know that there's more to a person than what she wears, but when you look good, you feel good, and feeling good gives you the confidence to do anything!

Knowing what boots go with your new mini or what belt looks best with your favorite pair of jeans isn't rocket science, but it does take some fashion know-how. And even if you already consider yourself a bit of a fashionista, you might still have days when you decide you hate your clothes and have nothing to wear. Welcome to your new fashion emergency kit!

for a Style Shake-up?

Style Trix for Cool Chix will help you get organized, get creative, and approach your closet with a whole new eye. You'll learn what clothes look best on your body type, the five items your wardrobe can't do without, and how to pull together a fabulous outfit at a moment's notice. You'll get tips on shopping like a pro, keeping your stuff organized, and choosing the right colors. And because fashion today is all about having cool stuff no one else has, there are even twelve projects for making and revamping your own unique clothing and accessories.

Armed with the tips in this book, you'll find that getting gorgeous in the morning takes less time than instant-messaging your best friend—and you'll leave the house looking better than Paris Hilton and Sarah Jessica Parker combined!

Sort

It Out

The first step to getting your look together is to see what you've got. Is your closet a disaster area and most of your stuff piled on the floor? If so, how can you know what you have? You've got to be able to reach in there and *see* if your pastel cardigan goes with your favorite baby blue tee, or if your purple jacket is so much better. If being able to find both shoes without digging around for fifteen minutes sounds too good to be true, it's time to give your closet an all-out makeover. So how do you do it? Just turn the page and let us show you the way.

What's Your Closet IQ?

When it comes to style, are you organized to the point of being obsessed? Or are there items in your closet that haven't seen the light of day for years? Find out how bad your style situation really is with this easy quiz.

1. How would you describe your closet?

A) It's a living nightmare. I can't see what's at the bottom, there's stuff spilling out onto the floor, and I can't figure out which is my dirty laundry pile and which is my "to fold" pile!

B) It's pretty neat. Every once in a while I get rid of old stuff I know I'll never wear again, and I keep clothes in sections (like pants, skirts, and sweaters) so I can find them easily.

C) Not bad, but it needs work. It isn't exactly a mess, but it certainly isn't organized.

2. Do you plan your outfits the day before?

A) Yes. I put a lot of thought into my appearance and always plan the next day's outfit.

B) Are you kidding? I usually wear whatever I can find that's clean and doesn't have holes in it!

C) I think about it a little, but I don't plan it exactly. I pretty much just rotate the same basic outfits each week.

3. How do you feel about shopping?

A) It's one of my favorite things to do! But even though I buy a lot of stuff, I still feel like I have nothing to wear.

B) I only shop when I need something, or to replace something that's worn out.

C) I like to shop, but I get overwhelmed and have trouble finding what I really need.

4. Do you know exactly what's in your closet?

A) No. I only wear what I can find right away. How am I supposed to remember what's all the way in the back?

B) Pretty much. But there's a bunch of stuff in there that I never wear.

C) Yes. I know exactly what I have and where it is.

5. Where do you keep your shoes?

A) On racks. I keep them in good condition and make sure they're always clean.

B) In a row on my bedroom floor. Sometimes they get in my way, but at least I don't lose them!

C) In a pile at the bottom of my closet, under my bed, or on the floor. Half of them are way old, but I never have time to sit down and get rid of the scary ones.

6. Are you into accessories?

A) What accessories? They're the last things I think about when I'm rushing to get ready!

B) Sort of. I have some necklaces somewhere, but I keep them in all different places and it's a pain to remember where they are when I need them.

C) Yes! I keep my belts and scarves together in a basket on my dressing table, but they get a little tangled sometimes.

Your score

1. A) 1 B) 3 C) 2
2. A) 3 B) 1 C) 2
3. A) 1 B) 3 C) 2
4. A) 1 B) 2 C) 3
5. A) 3 B) 2 C) 1
6. A) 1 B) 2 C) 3

6–10 points
You need help! It sounds like your image is being totally sabotaged by the mess that is your closet. There is a fashion goddess in you struggling to get out, so turn the page immediately to find out how to free her.

11–14 points
You have a clue or two, but you're a long way from finishing the puzzle. Roll up your sleeves and get ready—giving your closet a makeover will give you the boost you need to kick your fashion factor up a notch!

15–18 points
You go, sister. We don't need to tell you the benefits of being organized! But even savvy fashion thinkers like you can get caught in a rut. Turn the page for tips on giving your closet a whole new look!

Out with the Old

It's easy to get attached to clothes—getting rid of worn-out faves can feel like saying good-bye to old friends. And what about those items in your closet with the price tags still attached? You know, like that orange camouflage skirt that looked so cool in the store but seemed ridiculous once you got it home? You can tell yourself that you'll get around to wearing those things one day, but if you're serious about having a closet full of clothes that you truly love, the pain of saying "C-ya!" to the rejects is so worth it.

Closet Checklist

Start by taking absolutely everything out of your closet and dumping it in a big pile on your bed. You'll also need three big boxes labeled "Keep," "Fix," and "Out of here." The number-one rule for a killer closet makeover is simple: if you haven't worn it in the past year, it's time to kiss it good-bye. Take a good look at everything and go through this checklist:

1. Take an item from the pile. Apply the "have-I-worn-this-in-a-year?" rule. If the answer is no, put it in the "Out of here" box. If it's yes, move on to the next question.

2. Does it fit and look good? An honest friend will be a huge help here. Try not to get offended. After all, don't you want to know if it *really* looks good? If the item doesn't make you feel great, put it in the "Out of here" box.

3. If the item needs fixing or cleaning, put it in the "Fix" box. Promise yourself that you'll deal with that box soon.

4. If the item is ready to wear, into the "Keep" box it goes!

5. Stuff you haven't worn recently or that doesn't fit anymore hits the "Out of here" box.

"Trash or Treasure" Party

So what happens to the clothes in the "Out of here" box? It's completely up to you. You can donate them to charity, or throw a "Trash or Treasure" party with some friends. Everyone brings clothes they don't wear anymore, then you sort through the goods and trade stuff or take your pick of what no one else wants. But be warned! The point of a party like this is to purge your closet, not wind up with more stuff than you started with, so think carefully about taking on someone else's unwanted clothes. Limit yourself to two or three pieces, just to make it fun. At the end of the party, take what's left to a homeless shelter or some other charity organization. That way your closet clean-out is all good —for you and for others, too!

So, What Have You Got?

Take everything out of your "Keep" box and put it in piles according to type—skirts in one pile, tees in another, and so on. When you start doing this, you might discover that you have lots of the same kind of item. For example, you may see that—hello!—you have four almost identical black hoodies. So what do you do? Keep the two you like best, give the others to charity, and make a note to yourself: "No more black hoodies!"

You'll probably also find items you forgot you had—seeing everything together like this is a great opportunity to think of new ways to wear things. Get a small notebook to write down outfit ideas. If you have items you love but you don't have anything to wear them with, jot down what you need. Next time you're shopping, you can focus on finding fab pieces to fill the gaps in your wardrobe.

Weekly Style Check

Now that you've whipped your closet into shape, promise yourself to keep it up! Once a week, when you are putting away your clean laundry, take a few minutes to make sure everything is where it should be. Has a white T-shirt found its way into your underwear drawer, or is your sweater section slipping from a neat, color-coded stack to a shapeless heap? Now's the time to take action!
Better to keep things in shape with a tweak here and there than have to do the whole job from scratch again!

Hang It Up

Once you have identified all the things that you love to wear, it's time to store them so you can put together the perfect outfit for any occasion at a moment's notice. Getting dressed is tons easier when you can find all your clothes! Oh, and always make sure that your things are clean and ironed before you put them away.

Dresses

If there's room, hang your dresses in the closet. Make sure the hems don't get caught on stuff at the bottom by clearing out any junk lurking there. Now put the dresses in groups: sundresses, formal dresses, and everyday dresses. Hang them without bunching them together and they'll stay neat and wrinkle-free.

Skirts

To keep wrinkles away, put your skirts on hangers (not crammed in a drawer)—this will also keep them front

and center where you can see them. Group them by type, like you did with your dresses, to keep all your options at your fingertips.

Shirts and Tops
Hang all your tops together, organized by type (except tees and other casual tops—those can go in drawers). Group together the items you wear to school, on weekends, for special occasions, etc.

Pants and Jeans
Everyday pants like jeans, cords, khakis, and cargo pants should be folded neatly and stacked on a shelf or in a roomy drawer. Put pants that

get wrinkled easily on hangers. It's a good idea to use the right kind of hanger—the wire ones can leave ugly creases. Instead, use wooden hangers that keep your pants hanging straight and ready to wear.

Tees and Hang-out Clothes
Comfy sweats, tees, sweaters, and hoodies don't need to be hung up—but they shouldn't be twisted in balls at the back of your closet, either. Basic items like these should be folded, stacked, and grouped by color in drawers, with the ones you wear most at the top.

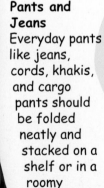

Accessories

Necklaces, scarves, belts, and hats are best hung from stick-on hooks on the back of your closet door. If you have a lot of stuff, it's a good idea to divide them by category—basic, funky, and formal—so each kind is in one place. Store jewelry like earrings and bracelets in small boxes or baskets on your dresser.

Shoes

From now on, always keep the box when you get a new pair of shoes. Keeping shoes in their boxes is the best way to keep them clean and dust-free. If you have an instant or digital camera, take a picture of each shoe and stick it to the outside of the box so you can see right away what's inside. If you don't have a camera, use a marker to write a description on the side of the box. If you don't have room in your closet for the boxes, buy a hanging shoe rack that fits over your closet rod—each pair of shoes fits in a separate compartment. Either way, you'll be able to see in an instant where your red sandals or blue sneakers are—and after all, who wants to waste precious time freaking out over a missing shoe?

Start Making Scents

For a finishing touch, keep your closet from smelling musty with some homemade scented sachets. Just cut a circle out of a piece of fabric and put a handful of dried lavender or potpourri (easy to find at a crafts or bath store) in the center. Gather up the material and tie it closed with a ribbon. A couple of these hanging up among your clothes will make everything smell pretty and fresh.

The Secrets to a

Girls come in all shapes and sizes. Think about it: do you have any friends with the exact same body type as yours? One of the most important style secrets is knowing what types of clothes look best on your unique shape. A skirt that looks adorable on your best friend isn't necessarily going to look amazing on you. That's why it's important to get to know what suits you—so that you can start to build up a collection of outfits that look great on *you*, not just on the hanger or in a magazine.

Killer Fit

What's Your Shape?

There are five general descriptions that fit most girls' body shapes. Everyone has something that makes her shape a little different, but these are loose categories that will help you figure out what clothes look best on your frame. Read the descriptions and check each statement that applies to you. When you're done, see which description has the most checks—that's your basic body type. If you have the same number of checks in two different descriptions, use both to guide your style choices. Then turn the page to discover how to make the most of what you've got!

Apple

- [ ] Your widest point is around your middle.
- [ ] Your shoulders are narrow.
- [ ] You have a bigger-than-average bust.
- [ ] Your chest area is wider than your shoulders.
- [ ] You have a small or flat butt.

Curvy

- [ ] You have a large bust.
- [ ] Your waist is well defined. Your figure definitely goes "in" here.
- [ ] Your hips are rounded.
- [ ] Your butt has a definite shape.
- [ ] Your legs are curvy.

Triangle

- [ ] You have broad shoulders.
- [ ] You have a curvy bust.
- [ ] You have thin hips.
- [ ] You have a small butt.
- [ ] You have long legs.

Beanpole

- [ ] You are skinnyish and your body is pretty much the same width all the way up and down.
- [ ] Your bust is small.
- [ ] Your hips are narrow.
- [ ] Your butt is small.
- [ ] Your legs are long and thin.

Pear

- [ ] You have narrow shoulders.
- [ ] You go "in" at the waist.
- [ ] Your hips are full.
- [ ] Your legs are short.
- [ ] You have a rounded butt.

Curvy
DOs and DON'Ts

• Don't be tempted to cover up your curves with baggy layers. They will make you look shapeless—not a great look!

• Do choose fitted clothes that show off your gorgeous "hourglass" shape. Fitted skirts and jackets will look great on you.

• Don't wear patterned skirts or pants. Keep them plain and go for prints up top instead.

• Do stock up on V-neck sweaters. They look amazing on your shape.

• Don't wear pants that taper at the bottom. These will do nothing for your shape.

• Do look for pants and jeans that are fitted on the hips but have wide legs.

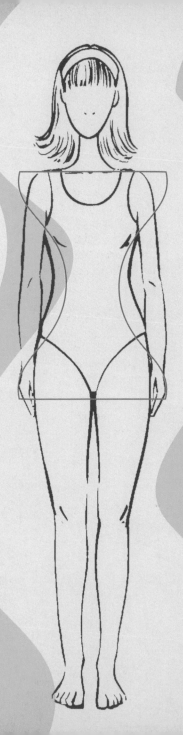

Beanpole
DOs and DON'Ts

- Don't make yourself seem longer than you are by wearing a full-length coat.

- Do wear a cute bomber jacket to keep you cozy and—most importantly—create a waist.

- Don't wear plain tops all the time.

- Do add shape to your top half with horizontal stripes.

- Don't forget to make the most of your model-like shape! You might not know it, but you are the envy of your friends.

- Do get a pair of skinny jeans. There's no body shape that these look better on!

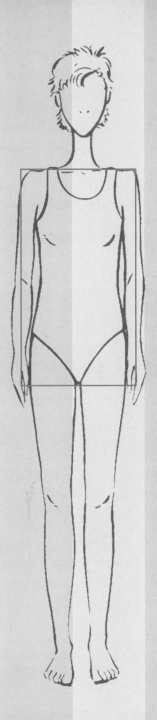

Triangle
DOs and DON'Ts

• Don't choose short, tummy-revealing tops that will make your top half look wider.

• Do choose longer tees and tops to make your top half seem longer and leaner. Pick tunic-style tops or off-the-shoulder styles to soften your shape.

• Don't go for big, chunky belts. These will make your shoulders look wide.

• Do pick patterned skirts and pants to draw the eye down and balance out your shape.

• Don't wear high-necked dresses that can make you look old-fashioned.

• Do go for slinky wrap dresses. They look great dressed up with heels or down with flip-flops and are the perfect shape for you.

Pear

DOs and DON'Ts

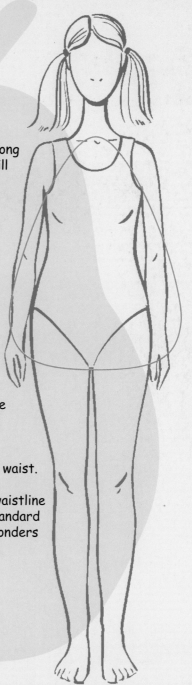

• Don't wear long skirts—they will overwhelm your shape.

• Do go for A-line skirts. They will make your hips look slim.

• Don't wear long jackets and coats that will widen your shape and make you look triangular.

• Do choose jackets with wide shoulders to balance out your lower half.

• Don't go for jeans with a high waist.

• Do wear jeans with a lower waistline (but not too low!) and with standard size pockets. They will do wonders for your butt!

Apple
DOs and DON'Ts

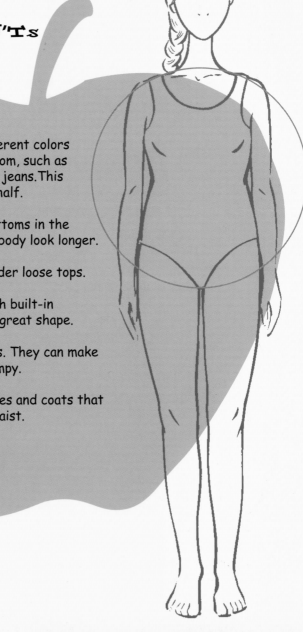

• Don't wear different colors on the top and bottom, such as a white tee with blue jeans. This will chop your body in half.

• Do choose tops and bottoms in the same color to make your body look longer.

• Don't hide your shape under loose tops.

• Do look out for tops with built-in waistbands—they give a great shape.

• Don't buy boxy coats. They can make your shape look stumpy.

• Do wear dresses and coats that go in at the waist.

The Rainbow Rules

We all have a favorite color, but have you ever thought about the colors you wear and how they affect the way you look? If you know the facts, you can use color cleverly to draw attention to or away from body parts and brighten your look. Read on to discover the secrets of the rainbow.

White

Only wear white on areas you want to stand out. The brightness will draw the eye to that area, so use it to your advantage by highlighting your fave body bits!

Black

Black is flattering on all skin tones and is well known for its slimming and smoothing qualities. The next time you're in an "I don't know what to wear" mood, pull on an all-black outfit and you'll be ready for anything.

Red

Red looks sensational on dark and black skins. For all other skin tones, it's great when you feel a bit sad, shy, or low-energy. Wear it with black pants or jeans for a dramatic look that will instantly give you a lift.

Yellow

Yellow isn't an easy color to wear. Avoid it if you have a sallow skin tone, as it will bring out the yellow in your skin. However, it's a fantastic color to wear with a tan, so save it for the sunshine!

Brown

Think brown means boring? Think again! Consider it a softer version of black. Brown looks great with denim, too, so jeans addicts should stock up on brown tops and boots.

Pink

Pale girls should go for a hot pink top or tee when they feel pale and uninteresting. The color will reflect onto the face to give a rosy glow. Feeling girly? Then pink is the only color to wear!

Orange

A truly tropical choice, orange and peach hues look great on most girls. If you have red hair or very pale skin, though, these colors may not work for you.

Blue

Baby blue is the color for blonde, blue-eyed babes, and looks great on dark brunettes, too. Avoid navy blue, which tends to look a bit mom-ish. Try royal blues and turquoise shades instead to add a splash of color.

Mauve

A pretty pastel color like mauve is flattering for most skin tones, but beware its effect on rosy cheeks. It has a tendency to exaggerate the rosiness, so save it for days when you're feeling pale and washed-out.

Green

Green looks best on girls with fair skin tones and light hair. It is a striking color for redheads, as it shows off their flame-colored locks and peachy skin to perfection. Darker-skinned gals should choose minty or olive tones.

What
Do

You Need?

Now's the time to transform your wardrobe! Make your closet the kind of place where you can always find an outfit that will make you look and feel completely fantastic. You might already have tons of items that you love—but if you don't have anything to wear them with, they'll stay right where they are, unworn and unloved. Read on to find out how to complete your wardrobe and release the fashionista within!

Are You a Fashion Victim?

Is fashion something you don't care much about, or is it your entire life? Find out whether you're a fashion expert or victim with this easy quiz.

1. Within your group of friends, how do you rate in the style stakes? Are you:
A) The most stylish, of course! You are the fashion guru to whom everyone comes for advice.
B) Way down. You don't have a clue when it comes to fashion, and no one would ask your opinion on clothes.
C) About average. You like to look good and enjoy shopping, but you're certainly not obsessed!

2. You're off to the mall with your bud. What shoes do you wear?
A) The first ones you find, even if they're your brother's sneakers.
B) Strappy sandals. They might be killing you after an hour, but there's no way you'd be seen out looking less than fabulous.
C) Your cute new sneakers. They're really comfy and you adore the way they look, too.

3. There's a party coming up and everyone you know is going. What are you planning to wear?
A) You're going shopping for a top to go with your favorite skirt.
B) No idea. You'll probably decide that night, but one thing's for sure—it will be comfy!
C) You've been saving for a dress in the chic-est boutique in town. Who cares if you only wear it once? It's so worth it.

4. While out shopping, you spot a dress you like. The problem is, it's really similar to one you already have. Do you buy it?
A) No way. You barely buy any clothes at all, so why double up?
B) No. It's tempting—so cute! But you know it's better to save the cash for something you need.
C) Of course! After all, you've worn the other dress twice and everyone's already seen it!

5. Where do you get your fashion advice and inspiration?

A) Fashion magazines. You take in every word and copy the styles for yourself.

B) You judge an item by how comfy it is.

C) You love magazines, but you like to be individual, too, so you don't take them too seriously.

Your score

Add up your score to find your fashion attitude!

1. A) 3 B) 1 C) 2
2. A) 1 B) 3 C) 2
3. A) 2 B) 1 C) 3
4. A) 1 B) 2 C) 3
5. A) 3 B) 1 C) 2

1-5 points

You certainly don't lose any sleep over style, do you? Comfort is all that matters to you. But why not spread your wings and try out some new looks? Who knows, you might enjoy fashion after all!

6-10 points

You have a great approach to style. You enjoy shopping and looking good, but there's no way you'd ever be a slave to fashion. You love your individuality too much to just follow the crowd!

11-15 points

You adore clothes and will do anything to wear the latest styles. It's great that you have something to be passionate about, but don't you think you might be taking the whole thing a bit too seriously? After all, fashion should be fun, and just one of many interests in life!

Getting the Basics

There are certain, basic items that every girl should have in her wardrobe. These things might seem ordinary and boring on their own, but it's with these key pieces that you can start to build your own unique style.

A Great Pair of Jeans

Denim is a girl's best friend. The right pair of jeans will look good in pretty much any situation, from a chilled-out study date with a friend to dinner out with your folks.

FIVE WAYS TO WEAR 'EM

1. Visit with Friends
Flat shoes and a gypsy top are all you need to turn your jeans from plain to pretty. Finish off the look with a bunch of bracelets.

2. Study Date
Keep it comfy with cool sneakers and your favorite tee. Add a hoodie to keep out the chill in cold seasons. A high ponytail or braids will keep your hair off your face while you're working, and you'll look cute, too!

3. Shopping Trip
Simplicity itself. A plain black tank or fitted V-neck sweater and black slip-on flats or pumps make an elegant outfit that is easy to change in and out of. What's more,

jeans are the perfect thing to wear when you're trying on tops and sweaters.

4. Beach Vacation
Roll up your jeans for a cute clamdigger style. A striped tee, flip-flops, and a sun hat complete the look.

5. Night Out
This is where your jeans really shine. Wear them with an evening top (think sequins, beading, or embroidery) and strappy sandals or boots, depending on the season. Add earrings and a glitzy belt.

A White Tee

Probably the most versatile item in your entire wardrobe! If possible, build up a collection with different necklines and sleeve lengths. Keep them nice and white and replace them if they start to turn yellow.

FIVE WAYS TO WEAR IT

1. Traveling
Pick a pair of cool slouchy pants that are comfy to sit in, then pull on your trusty tee. A knitted cardie is a pretty way to keep the chill out, especially if you're traveling by plane.

2. Out and About with Mom
Team your tee with cropped trousers and flat sandals. Pull your hair into bunches for a cute, hassle-free style that will keep your locks out of the way.

3. Garden Party
Have a floral skirt? Then you need a white tee! Busy patterns should always be teamed up with plain items, so these two make a perfect pair. Slip on some white sandals and you're ready to mingle.

4. Summer Hike
Khaki shorts are practical and comfy, and a cool white cotton tee looks perfect with them. White socks peeking out from your hiking boots complete your outdoorsy look.

5. City Visit
There are few outfits so classic and timeless as jeans and a crisp white tee. Low-heeled sandals or trendy sneaks will allow you to explore in comfort without sacrificing style.

A Pair of Black Pants

A dressier option than jeans, but just as comfortable, a great pair of black pants will save you from any style dilemma! They never go out of style and you can totally transform them with a little clever styling.

FIVE WAYS TO WEAR 'EM

1. First Date
A tube top and strappy sandals will make you feel super-sophisticated but comfier and less self-conscious than if you'd worn a dress. Plus, this neck-revealing look is a great chance to show off a fave necklace!

2. Job Interview
Track down a simple black jacket, and hey—it's a suit! Keep the look from being too grown-up by wearing a fun top underneath, and keep shoes black and simple.

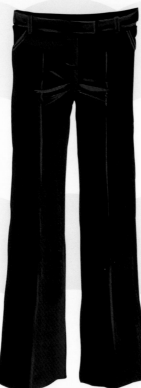

3. Winter Lunch
Keeping warm doesn't have to mean bulking up in thick sweaters. Wear wool tights under your pants and a skinny black tee under a slim-fitting black polo neck and you'll have a sleek but cozy silhouette. Boots with heels add extra sophistication.

4. When You Hate Everything in Your Wardrobe
Pull on a black tank or tee with your pants for an easy but cool outfit. Feel like shaking up the look? Then add brightly colored shoes or bracelets.

5. Swishy Dinner with the Parents
Team your pants with a shoestring-strap tank and smart flip-flops for a fun yet sophisticated look. Add silver jewelry if you feel too plain.

A V-neck Sweater

Think keeping warm is all about layers of baggy sweaters? Think again. A fitted V-neck sweater will keep you looking "put together" even on the chilliest days, and cotton versions can be worn to ward off the chill of summertime air-conditioning, too.

FIVE WAYS TO WEAR IT

1. Wintry Date
Cozy up the sweater with a bright scarf, wool skirt, and matching tights. Finish off with boots and you're set for a romantic walk in the snow.

2. Birthday Lunch
Team up your sweater with a denim miniskirt and strappy sandals. A pair of dangly earrings and matching bracelet will add festive touches for the celebration!

3. Lazy Sunday
Go for slouchy, low-waisted jeans and sneakers to look good and feel comfy while chillin' out, whether in front of the TV or at your grandma's.

4. Babysitting
You need a balance of looks for this one. With soft pants in a dark color or nice jeans, and flat slip-ons or sandals, you'll look smart and responsible but will still be able to run around with the kids.

5. Vacation
Summer evenings chillier than the days? Pull on your sweater over shorts and a plain tee for a cozy cover-up that's way nicer than a sweatshirt.

An A-Line Skirt

If you only buy one skirt, make it a simple A-line shape in a plain, dark shade. This flattering style is super-easy to wear and can be worn all year round in a zillion different outfits.

FIVE WAYS TO WEAR IT

1. Autumn Walk
A chunky roll-neck sweater is a great combo with a skirt like this. Don't forget to put on cozy tights and your favorite boots before you go out kicking leaves!

2. Summer Barbecue
Give your skirt a romantic look with a pretty top, like a pink tank in a flowery print. Light-colored sandals or flip-flops add to this breezy outfit.

3. Library Visit
A simple long-sleeved tee and cute moccasins make this skirt a comfy but feminine option for an everyday activity.

4. Beach
Team your skirt with colorful flip-flops and a tank. Luckily, a skirt like this is super-easy to pull on over your bikini! Add a shell necklace or anklet for a beachy feel.

5. Visiting Relatives
Add a floral shirt and flats for a cute outfit that won't have your mom sending you back to your room to change!

Shopping Like a Pro

Now that you know which essential items are missing from your wardrobe and you've figured out which shapes and colors suit you best, it's time to hit the mall. But successful shopping requires some advance preparation. With so many stores and so much choice, it's a wonder anyone manages to make any decisions at all! If you find the whole shopping experience bewildering and often end up buying stuff you'll never wear, it's time to perfect your shopping strategy.

Plan Ahead

Figure out what you need before you go. Remember back in chapter 1, when you were going through your stuff and writing down outfit ideas in your notebook? Now's the time to go back to that list. The items that spend their lives stuck in your closet deserve an outing every now and then, so think about what you need to make them into an outfit. There's a chance these unworn items might need one of the five key pieces from "Getting the Basics" on pages 44 to 49.

Set a Budget

Work out how much you have to spend and decide before you hit the mall what you need to spend it on. Allow more money for basic items, such as those in "Getting the Basics." These are things you will wear over and over, so you should buy the very best that you can afford. However, shopping should be enjoyable, so set aside a little cash for fun items or bargains you might discover as you look around.

Happy

Choose Your Perfect Shopping Buddy

This person should be honest, sensible, and—above all—stylish! If you like her look, you should listen to her advice. Be sure that this person is willing to spend time looking for stuff for you. In return, you can spend time another day helping her to shop.

Test the Fit

When you're in the changing room, use these simple tests to make sure an item really fits. With pants, sit down in them to make sure you have the right size and that they're comfortable. With tops, lift your arms to see if the fabric rides up. Walk around in the item for a few minutes to see how it looks and feels. Listen to your shopping buddy's opinion and not that of the sales assistant, who just wants to sell you stuff.

Try It On

When you see something you like, always try it on. Clothes have a way of looking totally different on your body than on the hanger. This can work both ways—you might find that something you thought was only okay actually looks sensational when you put it on. So remember—if in doubt, try it out!

Come Back Later

Use the "come back later" technique. You might feel you've found the perfect black tank, but a savvy shopper only buys when she's had a good look around the other stores. Only make the purchase at the end of the day—unless of course there's only one left in your size!

Decision Time

If you really can't decide whether you like something or not, don't get it. If an item is truly right for you and your style, your shopping sense will let you know!

Shopping!

5 Great

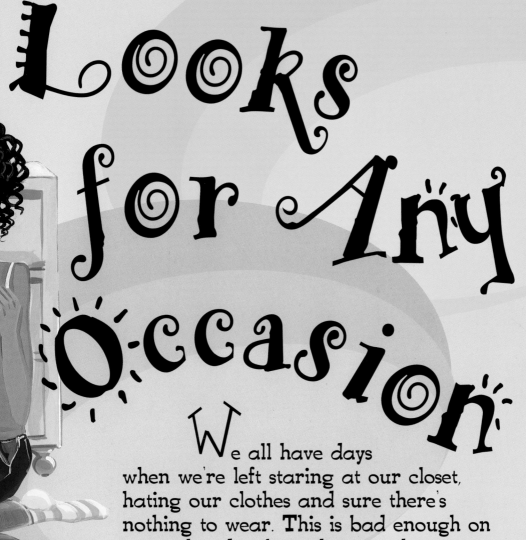

Looks for Any Occasion

We all have days when we're left staring at our closet, hating our clothes and sure there's nothing to wear. This is bad enough on a regular day, but when you have a date or an important event, it can be super-stressful. What you need is a stash of no-fail outfits that will look amazing and get you through any occasion. And that's exactly what you're going to get! With our five fashion cheat sheets you'll be ready to take on any style challenge and come out shining.

The first step on any given day is to think about what you want from your outfit. Does it need to be comfy, or can you be a little impractical? Do you want to blend into the background or stand out from the crowd? Each day, check out the boxes on pages 57 and 58 to see which is closest to the way you're feeling, then turn to the matching cheat sheet for inspiration.

Be Your Own Stylist

You want to look good in an easy, laid-back way. Comfort is key, but you don't want to sacrifice style. Sound right? If so, turn to

STYLE CHEAT SHEET

You're in a blissed-out, floaty mood and you want a look to match. You want to feel free and easy with a touch of flower child thrown into the mix. Follow your feeling to

STYLE CHEAT SHEET

You're in the mood for fun and want an outfit to match. This is not the time for a formal outfit—you want to look and feel dressed up, but in a funky, fashionable way. Let your fingers lead you to

STYLE CHEAT SHEET

Today is an important day. You have something to do and you want people to take you seriously. At the same time, you want to look supremely stylish, and you certainly don't want to be uncomfortable. If this is how you feel, turn to

STYLE CHEAT SHEET

You want to make an impact! Whether it's for a special date, a party, your graduation, or a dance, you want to look amazing. If this is you right now, turn to

STYLE CHEAT SHEET

3 4 5

THE LOOK:
Laid-back and comfy

Hair
Braids fastened with hair elastics that match the color of your hair. If you have thick or very curly hair, leave the ends loose for an even softer look.

Beauty
A healthy glow is your aim. Smooth a nude pink lipstick onto your lips, then smudge a little onto the apples of your cheeks.

Accessories
A chunky belt around your waist means you'll look "together" but still casual.

Outfit
Loose pants and fitted, layered tees. Add a zip-up hoodie in winter.

Feel Good
Get ready to go all day by giving yourself a foot massage in the morning. Mix a couple drops of peppermint essential oil into plain body lotion for a foot lotion that will relax your feet while waking them up, too!

Footwear
Cool sneakers

2

THE LOOK:
Hippie chick

Hair
Leave your hair long and flowing, or pick out your prettiest hair decoration. A flower or butterfly clip would be perfect.

Beauty
Highlight eyes with soft, pearly eye shadow in a light color.

Accessories
Tons of gold bracelets

Outfit
A pretty tiered skirt and a tie-dyed tube top. Add a crocheted shawl if it's chilly.

Feel Good
Slather yourself with a flowery, perfumed body lotion to feel totally feminine.

Footwear
Flat leather sandals or espadrilles

THE LOOK:
Funky fashion

Hair
A high-as-you-dare ponytail

Beauty
Colored eyeliner and clear lip gloss

Accessories
A single sparkly bangle

Outfit
Your best jeans and a cool evening top. Add a jean jacket on cold days.

Feel Good
Spritz yourself with an energizing fragrance before you head out on the town. Choose something with citrus notes for a zingy boost.

Footwear
Sparkly low heels or flip-flops

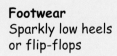

STYLE CHEAT SHEET

4

THE LOOK:
Cool and sophisticated

Hair
Smooth, poker-straight hair

Beauty
Keep it simple. Mascara and a clear lip balm are a great combination.

Outfit
Black pants and a black tee. On cold days, swap the tee for a fitted black turtleneck or V-neck sweater.

Accessories
None. This is all about simplicity.

Feel Good
An outfit like this calls for a calm, in-control outlook. Feeling frazzled? Take five deep breaths in and out and you'll feel instantly calmer.

Footwear
Black sneakers, flats, or flip-flops

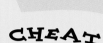

STYLE

CHEAT

SHEET

THE LOOK:
Dressed-up and romantic

Hair
Nothing says "special occasion" more than an up-do. Pull up your hair as if you were going to tie it into a pony, but twist it around and around until it twists into a knot. Use bobby pins to secure it in place.

Outfit
A pretty sleeveless dress. Think satin or beaded. A silky cardie will keep out the cold on a cool evening.

Beauty
Play up your eyes with smoky, charcoal-gray eye shadow.

Accessories
Sparkly earrings and a matching necklace

Feel Good
When you look this special, you have to walk tall. Pull your shoulders back for instant confidence and elegance.

Footwear
Strappy sandals with heels

Be Unique!

News flash! Style isn't about copying everyone else. It's about knowing what suits you and developing a look that's all your own. One of the easiest ways to do that is to get crafty! Customizing clothes and accessories or making them from scratch means you get to pick the colors and patterns, so you can guarantee no one else will have the same stuff. It's a great way to save money and be truly individual. What's not to love?

What's Your Style?

1. Your perfect Saturday night would be:
   A) Going to the opening night of an amazing new play.
   B) Sitting around a bonfire, guitar in hand, singing with your friends.
   C) Dancing like crazy at a friend's party.

2. When you lie in bed at night, what do you dream of?
   A) Getting invited to all the best parties and being the most popular girl in school.
   B) Working with animals and spending most of your time outdoors.
   C) Having your own shop full of gorgeous things.

3. If you described yourself as an animal, what would you be?
   A) A gorgeous peacock.
   B) A lucky ladybug.
   C) A fluffy Persian cat.

4. When you're stressed out, how do you like to relax?
   A) You light some candles, cuddle up in bed, and read your favorite book.
   B) You invite a bunch of friends over for a pamper-fest: face packs, foot massages, manicures—the works.
   C) You put on your iPod and crank up the tunes!

5. What's your everyday makeup look?
   A) You don't leave the house without base, blush, mascara, eyeliner, and a lip color.
   B) You rarely wear makeup.
   C) You wear pink lip balm and mascara.

6. On your birthday, what type of card does your best bud send you?
   A) A cute animal card.
   B) A stylish card with a fashion illustration on it.
   C) A rainbow card that she made herself.

Your score

Add up your score to find out which projects are right for you!

1. A) 2 B) 1 C) 3
2. A) 3 B) 1 C) 2

3. A) 3 B) 1 C) 2
4. A) 1 B) 2 C) 3

5. A) 3 B) 1 C) 2
6. A) 2 B) 3 C) 1

6–9 points
Hey hippie girl! You love nature and are attracted to all things that remind you of it. Your style should reflect your laid-back attitude to life. Check out the projects with the rainbow symbol.

10–14 points
You are feminine and floaty and love the romantic look. Make sure your style reflects the person within. Go straight to the projects with the flower symbol.

15–18 points
You are a girl who loves to party and be the center of attention. You adore fashion and go for the latest trends. Look for the handbag symbol—these are the projects most suited to you.

ALSO...
If you feel like shaking things up a little, why not try out one of the projects for the other style types? Who knows, it could be the start of a whole new you!

Finding Your Look

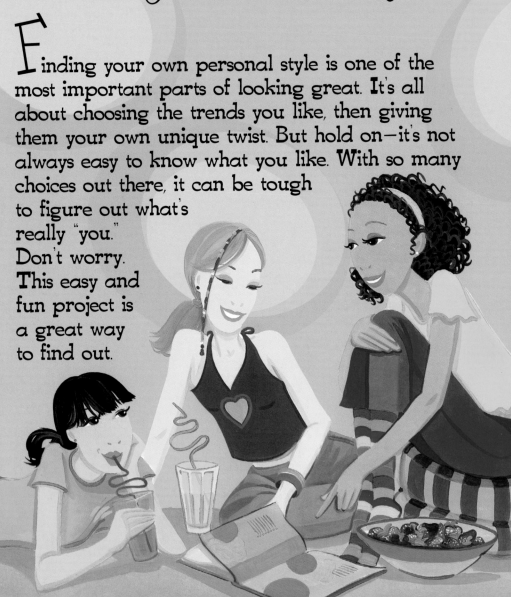

Finding your own personal style is one of the most important parts of looking great. It's all about choosing the trends you like, then giving them your own unique twist. But hold on—it's not always easy to know what you like. With so many choices out there, it can be tough to figure out what's really "you." Don't worry. This easy and fun project is a great way to find out.

Make a Style Idea Board

The next time you're flipping through a magazine, keep an eye out for items and looks you love and rip them out. Maybe it's a cute tote bag in an ad, the way your favorite celeb layers her tees, or even a color you like. Here are some things to look for:

colors you think would look good on you

ways to customize your clothes

new ways to wear old favorites

funky style ideas

things you want to make

stuff to look for next time you're shopping

looks you love

Start keeping a folder of all the stuff you've ripped out. Pretty soon you'll have a pile of pictures that reflect your personal taste. Does the same item or look crop up again and again? If so, you obviously love that style!

Get a big piece of posterboard and stick your pictures all over it with glue or tape. When you're done, put it up somewhere in your room where you can see it.

Just like fashion, your tastes will change pretty often, so make a new style board at the start of every season. This way, you'll always have a clear vision of what you truly love. Have fun!

Safety Pin Bracelet

This chunky bracelet will appeal to your arty side. It can be as bright or as delicate as you like, and it makes a great gift for a good friend.

1. Decide on the colors and types of beads for each safety pin. Play around with different designs until you're happy with your choice.

2. Open the first safety pin and slide on as many beads as will fit. Close the safety pin. Repeat with the other pins.

3. Take one piece of the elastic cord and tie a knot in the end. Slide on a small bead, then thread the elastic through the top of a beaded safety pin. Slide on a small bead. Now thread the elastic through the *bottom* of a beaded pin. Keep sliding on pin (top), bead, pin (bottom), bead, until all the pins are on the elastic.

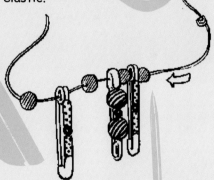

4. Get the other piece of elastic and repeat step 3 with the other end of the safety pins.

5. When you're done, tie the ends of each piece of elastic in a double-knot to secure. Then just slide on the bracelet!

Fancy Jeans

Denim is the perfect blank canvas for letting your creativity run riot. Give an old, unloved pair of jeans a makeover and they'll soon be your faves again!

You will need:

- colored pencils
- paper
- old jeans
- decorating material such as fabric paint, stick-on sequins, ribbon, glitter pens, fabric glue
- dressmaker's chalk or fabric pencil

1. Use colored pencils to design your dream jeans on a piece of paper. You might decide to make your jeans into a work of art with fabric paint, rows of sequins, or ribbon down the seams, or you could draw flowers in glitter. Keep the design simple for maximum impact.

2. Use the chalk or fabric pencil to carefully copy your design onto the jeans so you can get it just right.

3. Now do the designs for real. Decorate one side at a time and let the glue or paint dry before you do the other side.

4. Remember to check the glue or paint instructions before washing your new jeans to keep them looking fabulous!

73

Evening Clutch

This smooth little bag is so easy to make, you can whip one up to go with every outfit! There's just enough room inside to carry a lip gloss, mirror, keys, and a cash card.

You will need:

- pencil
- ruler
- PVC-coated cotton (this is usually used for tablecloths)
- sheet of paper
- fabric glue
- scissors

1. Measure out a piece of fabric the same size as a sheet of paper. Cut it out.

2. Measure 8 in. (20cm) up from the bottom of the fabric and draw a light pencil line. Fold the bottom up to meet this line. Use your fingers to make a crease along the fold. Now fold the top over to make a flap.

3. Open the fabric. Spread a line of glue along the inner edges of the bag (but not the top flap). Keep the line of glue as thin and close to the edge as possible.

4. Fold the bottom back up and press into the glue. Pile some heavy books on top and leave overnight to let the glue dry and set the creases of the bag.

Tie-Dyed Tee

Laid-back and very hippie-chick in style, this top has a genuine 1970s feel you'll love. Protect your clothes with an apron or old shirt before starting this project.

You will need:

- 1 plain white cotton tee
- rubber bands
- rubber gloves
- fabric dye in your favorite color
- packet of dye fix
- salt
- plastic bucket

1. Before you start, wash the tee (even if it's brand-new) and leave it damp. Any dirt on the fabric will prevent the dye from "taking" properly.

2. To make a swirl on the tee, grab a little fabric and wrap a rubber band really tightly around it. (The rubber band prevents the dye from coloring the fabric.) Repeat until you have enough swirls.

3. Put on the rubber gloves. Mix up the dye with the water, dye fix, and salt in a bucket. (Check the instructions on the packet for how much water and salt you'll need.)

4. Put the tee in the dye and swirl it around. Leave the tee in the bucket for an hour. Swirl it around occasionally for the first ten minutes, then just let it sit.

5. After an hour, take off the rubber bands and rinse the tee in cold water until the water runs clear. The instructions on the dye packet will tell you how to wash the tee to remove the extra dye.

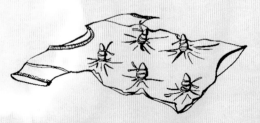

Sweet Shopper

Even functional things like shopping totes can be funky! This bag is simple to make and lots of fun to decorate.

You will need:

- 1 piece of plain fabric, 20 x 10 in. (50 x 25 cm)
- needle and thread
- gingham ribbon
- scraps of fabric
- fabric glue
- scissors

1. Fold the piece of fabric in half with the right sides together. Iron it flat.

2. Use a running stitch to sew up the two sides of the bag.

3. Fold the top edge over to make a hem and use a running stitch to secure.

4. Make handles with the gingham ribbon. Cut two pieces however long you want them. Sew the ends to the inside of the bag.

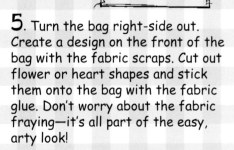

5. Turn the bag right-side out. Create a design on the front of the bag with the fabric scraps. Cut out flower or heart shapes and stick them onto the bag with the fabric glue. Don't worry about the fabric fraying—it's all part of the easy, arty look!

Ribbon Halter Top

Here's an easy way to give an old tee a second life—and get a gorgeous top for next to nothing!

You will need:

- 1 old tee that fits you snugly
- needle and thread
- ribbon 1 in. (2.5 cm) wide and about 5½ ft. (1 meter 65 cm) long in a contrasting color
- scissors

1. Carefully cut the arms and the neckband off the tee, as shown.

3. Thread the ribbon through both hems, making sure that the ends of the ribbon are equal lengths.

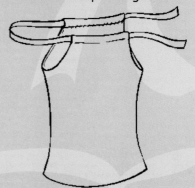

2. Fold over about 1 in. (2.5 cm) at the top of the new neck on each side and sew in place. Leave the ends open.

4. Slip on over your head, and tie the ends in a bow on one side.

Button Hat

These funky hats will appeal to all outdoorsy girls—they're both cozy and extremely cute.

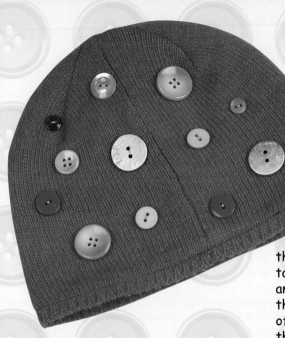

You will need:

- 1 plain wool pull-on hat
- buttons in different colors and sizes
- needle and thread
- scissors

1. Design your pattern. You can sew buttons all over the hat, in a line around the rim, or however you want.

2. Carefully thread the needle. Pull the thread until both ends are equal. Make a double-knot at the end, leaving a tail about 1 in. (2.5 cm) long.

3. Hold the first button where you want it to lie. Bring the needle inside the hat to just under the button and push it through the fabric and one of the holes in the button. Keep pulling the needle until the thread stops. Pass the needle through another hole to the inside of the hat, again pulling the thread taut. Repeat several times until the button is attached firmly.

4. Turn the hat inside out. Tie the tail and the long thread together in a knot to secure, then snip off the extra thread.

5. Repeat steps 3 and 4 to sew on all of the buttons. (Don't forget to double-knot the end of the thread before starting each new one.) The more you do, the speedier you'll become!

Bow Belt

This belt will add a pretty, romantic touch to even the plainest of outfits. You might want to make a few belts in different colors, or use striped or flowery ribbon.

You will need:

- ribbon 2 in. (5 cm) wide and about 40 in. (1 meter) long
- needle and thread
- piece of Velcro, 1 in. (2.5 cm) wide and 2 in. (5 cm) long
- fabric glue
- scissors

1. Hold the ribbon around your waist to measure how much you'll need. Add an extra 4 in. (10 cm), then cut it off at that length.

2. You'll need to seal the ends of the ribbon to keep them from unraveling. Turn the cut edge under and hem it.

3. Create a fastening by using fabric glue to attach the Velcro to the belt so that it closes on the overlap.

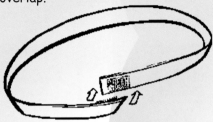

4. Make a big, fat bow with the leftover ribbon. Seal the cut edges as in step 2. Add a few stitches in the center of the bow to keep it from coming undone.

5. Attach the bow to the belt with a few stitches in the center. It should go on the end of the belt that will overlap the other, inside end.

Bejeweled Choker

Make like a millionaire with this super luxe choker. Pair it with a little black dress for an extremely special occasion.

You will need:

- velvet ribbon, 1 in. (2.5 cm) wide and 12 in. (30 cm) long
- fabric glue
- piece of Velcro, 1 in. (2.5 cm) wide and 2 in. (5 cm) long
- assorted plastic jewels with flat backs
- scissors

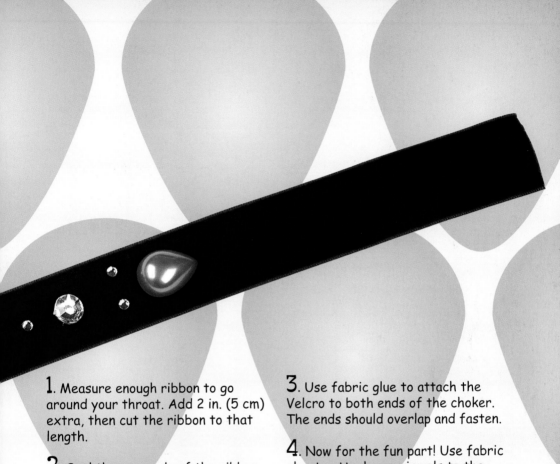

1. Measure enough ribbon to go around your throat. Add 2 in. (5 cm) extra, then cut the ribbon to that length.

2. Seal the raw ends of the ribbon by folding them over and sewing with a needle and thread (as described in "Bow Belt," page 84).

3. Use fabric glue to attach the Velcro to both ends of the choker. The ends should overlap and fasten.

4. Now for the fun part! Use fabric glue to attach your jewels to the choker. Go for a classic diamond design with clear jewels, or use multicolored gems for a funky look.

Twinkle Toes

Plain old shoes won't do anything for the soul of a true rainbow girl. Create some fab sparkly footwear that will match your style and add a spring to your step.

You will need:

- pencil
- pair of plain ballet shoes
- 2 packets of small, self-adhesive jewels (available from craft stores)
- fabric glue (optional)
- tubes of fabric paint in assorted colors

Hint

It's a good idea to practice making dots on a piece of paper first, so you can get a feel for how much paint to squeeze out of the tube.

1. Use the pencil to lightly mark on the shoes where you want to stick your gems.

2. When you're happy with the design, carefully press the self-adhesive jewels onto the shoes. (Add a dot of glue to any jewels that aren't sticking.)

3. Turn each jewel into a tiny flower by placing dots of paint around it. Make extra flowers with dots of one color paint surrounded by "petals" in a second color.

3. Keep going until both ballet shoes are decorated. Let them dry overnight, then slip them on and hit the town!

Twisty Bracelet

This bracelet is made with super-strong "memory" wire that comes already curled into loops. One roll of wire will give you enough to make plenty of bracelets!

You will need:

- needle-nose pliers
- 1 x 1 oz. (20 g) roll of memory wire or 3 single loops
- 1 oz. (20 g) green beads
- 1 oz. (20 g) blue beads
- 40 silver beads
- 10 heart-shaped turquoise beads
- 10 heart-shaped silver beads

Hint

If you don't have needle-nose pliers, you can start and finish the bracelet by sticking a small bead to the end of the wire with strong glue.

1. The needle-nose pliers have a small cutting tool on them. Use it to cut a length of wire. We have used three loops and allowed a bit extra for the ends.

2. Use the needle-nose pliers to bend one end of the wire into a small loop. This will keep the beads from sliding off.

3. Thread the beads onto the wire in whatever pattern you choose. Shake them down the wire from time to time. Take care when threading beads on the wire, as the cut end may be quite sharp.

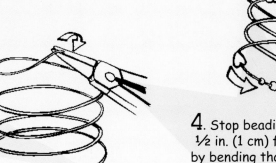

4. Stop beading when you get about ½ in. (1 cm) from the end. Finish by bending that end with the pliers as you did in step 2.

Glam Wrap

You'll feel totally fabulous in this snug faux-fur wrap. Throw it on and act like the starlet you are!

You will need:

- fake fur fabric, about 1 yard (1 meter) long and 1 ft. (30 cm) wide
- pencil
- large gold button
- needle and thread
- scissors

3. Make a buttonhole in the front of the wrap. To do this, carefully cut a slit the same length as the button's width in the top corner of one end of the wrap. Put the wrap around your shoulders to find the perfect place for the button, then sew it on using the instructions in "Button Hats" (page 83).

1. The wrap needs to be long enough to reach around your shoulders and fasten with a 2-in. (5-cm) overlap at the front. Carefully cut the fabric to the correct length and width. Faux fur fabric does not need hemming.

2. Place the wrap fur-side down on a work surface and draw a curve at each end of the wrap. Cut along the lines.

In-a-Minute Style Savers

Want to shake up your look but don't have time for one of our amazing projects? Never fear. Here are some speedy ideas for putting your own personal stamp on any outfit.

Safety Pins

Big safety pins are perfect for giving your favorite tee a punk feel without having to attack it with scissors. Use one safety pin on each sleeve to scrunch up the fabric, or gather some fabric together at the front of the tee and secure with a pin.

Ribbon and Lace

Pretty up any outfit with some glam-girl trimmings. Lengths of ribbon can be worn tied around your neck in a cute bow as a simple choker. Wide bands of lace make great retro-style cuffs for your wrists.

Scarves and Ties

Long silk or chiffon scarves and men's ties make super-funky belts, especially when worn with your coolest jeans. You can also tie a scarf around your head to give your whole look a hippie feel.

Pins and Jewelry

Accessories can change the look of an outfit in an instant. Raid your mom's jewelry box (with her permission, of course) for brooches or beads. Think they're too old-fashioned? It's all in the way you wear them. Pin a jeweled brooch onto a woolly hat or the front pocket of your jeans. Long strings of beads or pearls are perfect for winding around and around your wrists.

Think Different!

Give your look a lift without adding anything at all. Just wear a fave item differently and see how you like it! For example, if you always wear your jean skirt with flats, try it with boots. Or experiment with layering—a sundress worn over jeans as a tunic-style top can look seriously funky. Don't be afraid to experiment with clothes. If it doesn't look good, all you have to do is change!

Index